JAMES DUNN's family comes from Scotland, Ireland, England and Wales. He grew up in the Scottish Highlands and lives in North London, where he works in publishing. His other title for Frances Lincoln is *ABC UK*.

KATE SLATER grew up on a farm in Staffordshire and studied illustration at Kingston University. Kate works both in flat collage and also a combination of collage and paper-cuts which she uses to create suspended, relief illustrations. Kate likes hats, being high up, visiting schools, making jam, writing to-do lists and wearing other people's jumpers. She thinks being an illustrator and author is probably the best job in all the world, so she is very, very lucky.

For Hector and Aurora with love and thanks to Phoebe — J.D.
For Ronley, with love — K.S.

Frances Lincoln Children's Books,
74-77 White Lion Street, London, N1 9PF
www.franceslincoln.com

First published in 2012 by Frances Lincoln Children's Books
This edition published in paperback in 2013

ISBN: 978-1-84780-495-2

Text © James Dunn 2012
Illustration © Kate Slater 2012

The rights of James Dunn to be identified as the author and of Kate Slater to be identified
as the illustrator of this work have been asserted by them in accordance with the
Copyright, Designs and Patent Act, 1988.

A CIP catalogue record for this book is available from the British Library.

3 5 7 9 8 6 4 2

Printed in China

ABC
LONDON

James Dunn
Illustrated by Kate Slater

F

FRANCES LINCOLN
CHILDREN'S BOOKS

A is for
Art

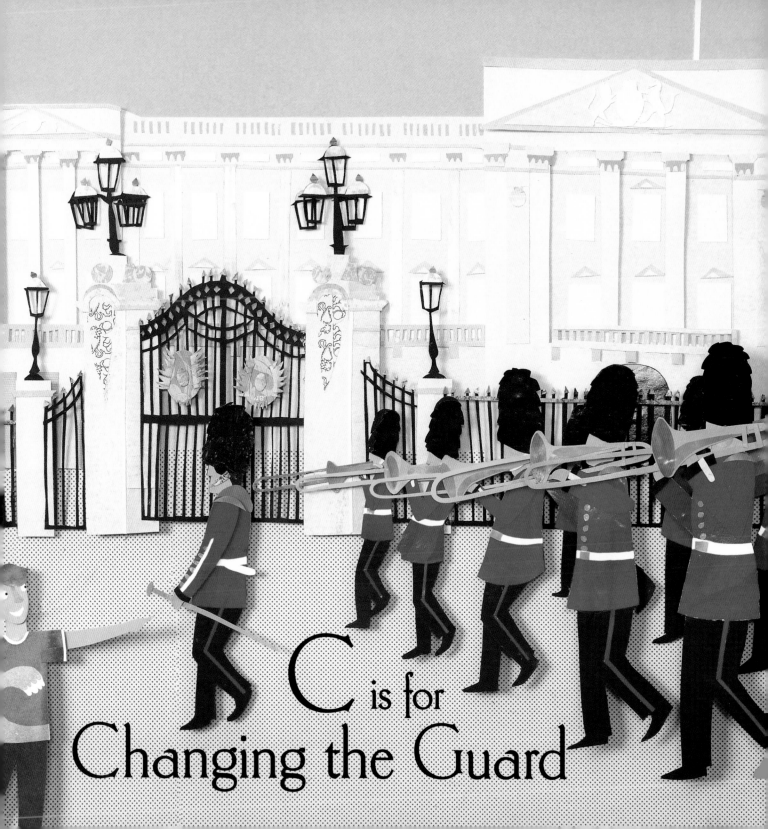

C is for
Changing the Guard

D is for
Dick
Whittington

E is for Elephant and Castle

G is for **Gherkin**

H
is for
HAMPSTEAD HEATH

I IS FOR ISLE OF DOGS

J is for

Jewels

K is for King's Cross

King's Cross

L IS FOR LIONS

M IS FOR
MUSEUM

N is for **Number 10**

is for

Observatory

P is for **PORTOBELLO ROAD**

Antiques

R is for

RIVER THAMES

S IS FOR **ST PAUL'S CATHEDRAL**

U is for
Underground

UNDERGROUND

WHITECHAPEL

Y is for

NEW
SCOTLAND
YARD

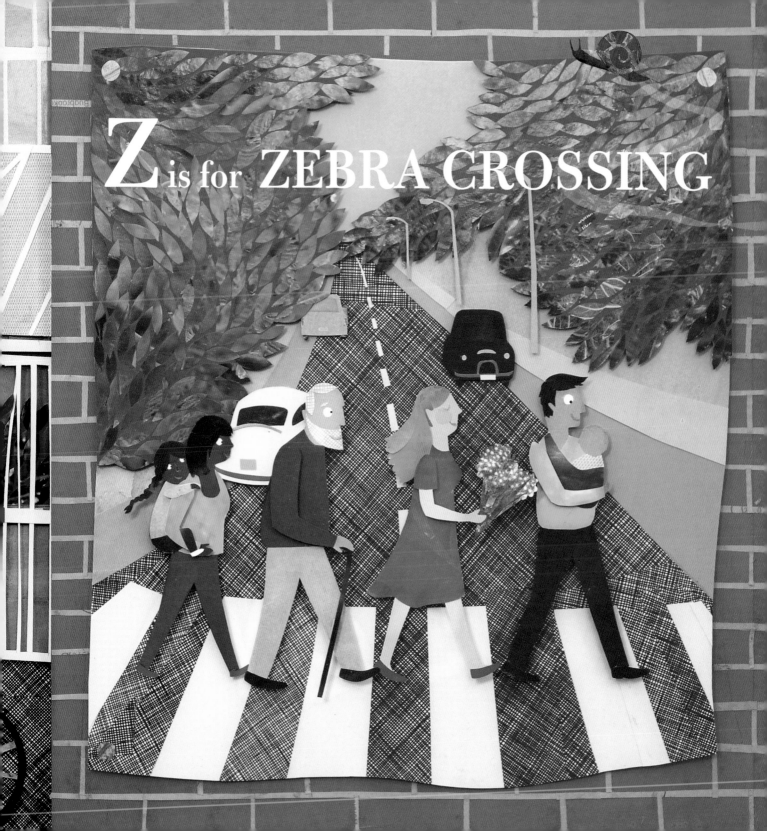

ALPHABET GLOSSARY

Art and artists are everywhere in London – in museums, galleries like Tate Modern and on the street.

People come from all over the world to visit the city or start a new life. You can see them in action (and get a great beigel) in **BRICK LANE**.

You have to concentrate when you're guarding the Queen. At Buckingham Palace soldiers take over guard duty in a ceremony called Changing the Guard.

Dick Whittington came to London a long time ago to make his fortune. He nearly quit the city, but ended up as Lord Mayor – after selling his cat for a lot of money because it was so good at getting rid of rats!

'Elephant and Castle' is how Londoners used to say *Infanta de Castilla*. She was a Spanish princess who married an English king, and this is where her palace once stood.

Fashion followers worldwide check out what Londoners are wearing on the street, and what London designers are doing on the catwalk.

Of all London's tall buildings, the easiest to recognise is the **Gherkin** at St Mary Axe.

HAMPSTEAD HEATH is a great wild open space on the hills to the north of the city. Lucky Londoners live in one of the greenest cities in the world.

The Isle of Dogs was once an island in the heart of London's docks – and is now home to a financial centre called Canary Wharf.

The *Crown Jewels*, bling for kings (and queens) – they're all locked up in the Tower of London.

King's Cross Station is where you catch a train to the North, or to Hogwarts. . .

LIONS roam everywhere in London. There are over 10,000 statues of them, like these ones in Trafalgar Square.

If you want amazing treasures, lost civilizations, awesome technology and huge dinosaurs, then head for a London MUSEUM, like the Natural History Museum in this picture.

Number 10 Downing Street is the address of the Prime Minister. He (or sometimes she) runs the government from here.

The Royal Observatory, Greenwich, is where the world sets its clocks. There's a Planetarium too.

Portobello Road is the most famous street market in London. From avocados to antiques, you can buy it all at Portobello.

What is the fairest way to wait for something? Queue – as everyone does here at the London Eye.

The **River Thames** links the heart of England to the rest of the world. London is the last place where you can cross the river before you reach the sea.

ST PAUL'S is London's own cathedral. Christopher Wren rebuilt it after the Great Fire of 1666.

TAXI drivers in London have brains stuffed full of 'the Knowledge' – how to get you to any street you ask for.

Underground trains carry Londoners on a billion journeys across their city every year. Stations all have the same distinctive circular symbol.

Villains have always made a killing in London. Hold on to your wallet!

Wimbledon is where you'll see the All England Tennis Club and the world's favourite tennis tournament each summer.

EXiles sometimes find a home in London when their own country won't let them stay. Some, like Karl Marx, have famous memorials.

The Metropolitan Police work to keep the city safe, from their headquarters at NEW SCOTLAND YARD.

At **Zebra Crossings**, traffic has to stop to let you cross the road. The most famous one, in Abbey Road, is on the cover of a Beatles album.

OTHER PICTURE BOOKS IN PAPERBACK FROM FRANCES LINCOLN CHILDREN'S BOOKS

ABC UK
James Dunn
Illustrated by Helen Bate

Find out about all things British in this Amazing, Brilliant, Creative alphabet celebration of the UK and its vibrant cultural identity.

BATTY
Sarah Dyer

No one notices Batty hanging upside down at the zoo. But trying to join in with the penguins, the gorillas and the lions is not for him. It's only when he returns to the bat enclosure that he makes a surprising discovery about what he is really good at.

BUBBLE TROUBLE
Margaret Mahy
Illustrated by Polly Dunbar

When Mabel blows a bubble so big that Baby accidentally floats away in it, the townsfolk come together to try and get him down safe and sound. A hilarious rhyming story, perfect for reading aloud.

Frances Lincoln titles are available from all good bookshops.
You can also buy books and find out more about your favourite titles,
authors and illustrators on our website: www.franceslincoln.com